HANS CHRISTIAN ANDERSEN'S
THE
Princess
-AND THE-
Pea

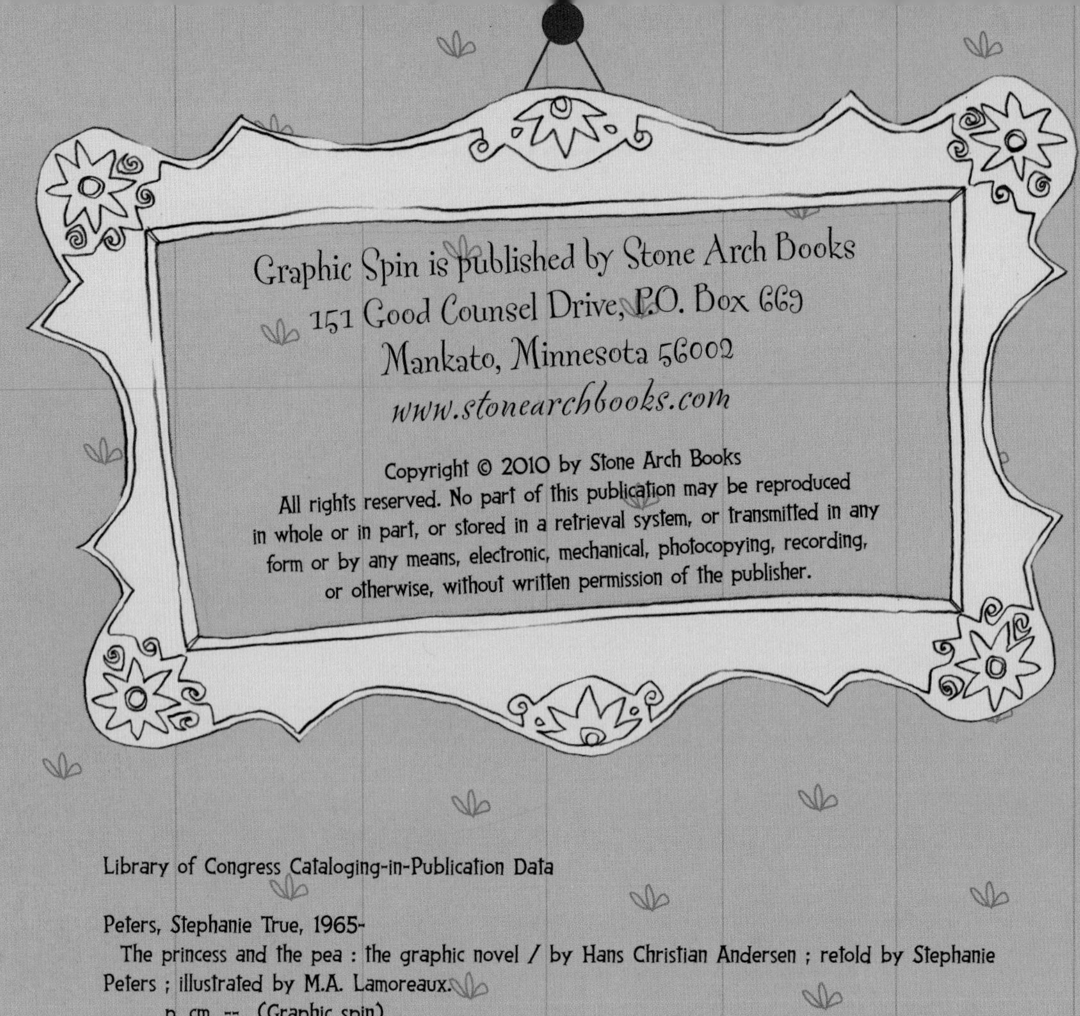

Library of Congress Cataloging-in-Publication Data

Peters, Stephanie True, 1965-
The princess and the pea : the graphic novel / by Hans Christian Andersen ; retold by Stephanie Peters ; illustrated by M.A. Lamoreaux.
p. cm. -- (Graphic spin)
ISBN 978-1-4342-1594-9 (library binding) -- ISBN 978-1-4342-1743-1 (pbk.)
1. Graphic novels. [1. Graphic novels. 2. Fairy tales.] I. Lamoreaux, M. A., ill II. Andersen, H. C. (Hans Christian), 1805-1875. Prindsessen paa aerten. III. Title.
PZ7.7.P44Pr 2010
741.5'973--dc22

2009010529

Summary: As a young prince nears adulthood, the queen tells him he must find a princess bride -- but not just any princess will do. Only a true princess will satisfy his mother. The young prince searches the entire kingdom, but returns home alone and sad. Late one stormy night, a mysterious woman knocks at the castle door. She claims to be a true princess, but the queen has her doubts. So, she concocts a clever scheme to see if the princess is the real thing.

Creative Director: Heather Kindseth
Graphic Designer: Emily Harris

Printed in the United States of America

HANS CHRISTIAN ANDERSEN'S

THE Princess -AND THE- Pea

The Graphic Novel

retold by Stephanie Peters
illustrated by M.A. Lamoreaux

STONE ARCH BOOKS
MINNEAPOLIS SAN DIEGO

Cast of Characters

The King

The Queen

The Princess
The Prince

Once upon a time, a prince was born to a wealthy king and queen.

The queen wanted only the best for her child.
This bed is too lumpy. Please find the prince a different one.
I like this one, Mama!

When the time came for the prince to marry, the queen insisted that he marry a princess.
But not just any princess. You must marry a *true* princess.
A *true* princess?
True princesses were very rare. So the prince left the next morning to travel the world in search of one.
Good-bye, dear son!
Good-bye!
But how will I know a true princess when I see one?

After a few days of traveling, the prince met his very first princess.
She's so lovely! She must be a true princess.

But then . . .
CRASH
I have a hair out of place! Fix it, you fools! Quickly!

I can see you have more important things to do, so I'll just be on my way.

The second princess he met seemed promising at first . . .
Moss always grows on the north side of trees. Did you know that?
I did not! How interesting!

But several hours later, he changed his mind.
You didn't know that some flowers grow from seeds and others from bulbs?
Or that turtles hatch from eggs, like chickens do?
You don't know anything, do you?

I do know one thing – I'm leaving!

Sadly, the prince didn't meet a true princess the next day . . .
Ha! My bouquet is prettier than yours!
My crown has more jewels!
I can stand on one foot longer than you!

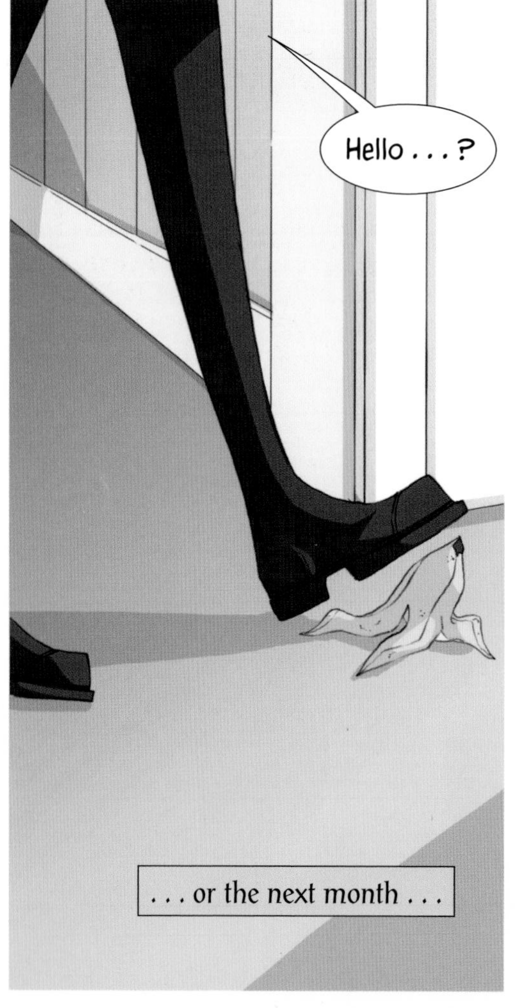
Hello . . . ?
. . . or the next month . . .

Hee hee!

. . . or the next year.

Ahem . . .
MUNCH
MUNCH

May I try some of this?

Don't touch that!
Or that!
It's mine! It's all mine!

Eventually, the prince quit his search and returned home.
Rest now, my dear boy. We'll talk in the morning.
I don't believe true princesses even exist!

The prince hadn't been asleep for long when a bright flash woke him.
CRACK
Ah!

I would hate to be outside on a night like this!

Suddenly, there was a loud pounding at the castle door.
BOOOOOM!
BOOOOM!
BOOOOOM!
Who is it, Father?
I'm not sure . . .
Who are you?

Just then, a young woman stepped into the light.
The queen was not impressed.
She's beautiful!
Are you a beggar?

I am not a beggar.
Rustle Rustle

I'm a princess.

Ha!
A liar is what you are.
I am not a liar!
Why were you out in this storm?
Well, it's kind of a long story . . .
"My father rules a small kingdom not far from here."
"I was out riding when I saw a strange bird flying overhead."

"As I tried to identify the bird,
I didn't notice the snake . . . "

". . . until it was too late."

"My horse fled, but
I didn't dare move."
"When the snake slithered away, I
stumbled onward, lost and alone."

"Then a bolt of lightning
illuminated your castle . . . "

. . . and here I am.
What an unbelievable story!
Quite unbelievable, indeed.

I think she's telling the truth! She's a true princess!

The queen didn't believe the girl was actually a princess, let alone a true one.
But she remained silent.
Instead, she set out to prove that the girl was lying.

She told a servant to find the girl some clean clothes.
I will have the cook fix us a special supper!

I am afraid I won't be joining you for dinner . . .

But I will make sure that a *special* bedroom is prepared for you.

The princess exchanged her muddy dress for a beautiful silk gown.

Green is my favorite color!
Mine too!

This is my favorite meal!
Mine too!

zzzZZZZZZ
After dinner, the prince read to the princess while the king dozed.

This is my favorite story!
Mine too!

It feels like I've known you my whole life.
Me too.

Meanwhile, the queen prepared the princess's bed.
Remove this mattress.
Then, fetch me twenty mattresses and feather beds to put in its place.

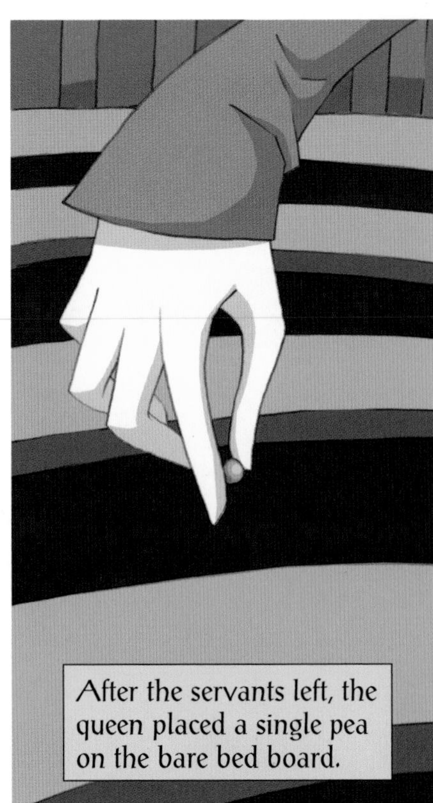
After the servants left, the queen placed a single pea on the bare bed board.

One by one, twenty mattresses were placed on top of the pea, followed by twenty feather beds.
We'll soon see how true this princess really is.

Afterward, the queen showed the princess to her bedroom.
Off you go, my son. A princess needs her beauty sleep.
Goodnight! I'll see you in the morning!

My goodness! Is that where I am to sleep?
Of course! A true princess deserves nothing less.

It was quite a climb to the top.
Good night, your Highness.
Sleep well, my dear.

I – I am
sure I will.
Oh, I'm
sure you
will too.

But the princess did not sleep well.
She tossed and she turned.
But she simply could not get comfortable.

These mattresses must be stuffed with rocks!
When morning came . . .
Owww . . . I think I've bruised my back.

The weary princess slowly made her way downstairs to join the others for breakfast.

How did you sleep?
Soundly, I'm sure.

I don't mean to sound ungrateful . . .

. . . but I didn't sleep a wink!

You . . . didn't?
Then that can mean only one thing . . .
You really are a true princess!

The queen then told them of her little test.
Only a true princess would possess the delicacy and sensitivity to feel a pea through forty mattresses.

Having heard his mother's approval, the prince didn't wait a second more . . .
My dear, *true* princess . . .

. . . will you marry me?

With all my heart, yes!

The prince and princess were married the very next day.
And, like two peas in a pod, they never left each others' sides.
The queen was also quite pleased.
And they lived together happily for the rest of their days.

As for the pea that proved the princess was true, it was given a place of honor in the Royal Museum, where it can still be seen today . . .

Sniff
Sniff
. . . unless, of course, it has been stolen!

About the Author

Hans Christian Andersen

April 2, 1805 – August 4, 1875

Hans Christian Andersen was born in Odense, Denmark. His parents were very poor, but they encouraged young Hans to write, act, and sing. With their help, Hans built himself a small theatre for his puppets so he could put on plays to entertain his family and friends.

As Hans grew up, he tried many different professions, but none of them seemed to fit. He eventually found work as an actor and singer, but when his voice changed, he could no longer sing well enough to make a living. Soon after, a friend suggested that he start writing. A short time later, he published his first story, "The Ghost at Palnatoke's Grave."

Andersen's first book of fairy tales was published in 1835. Andersen adored children, so most of his fairy tales focused on them. He continued to write children's stories, publishing one almost every year, until he fell ill in 1872.

Andersen had written more than 150 fairy tales before his death in 1875. His stories have been translated into more than 150 different languages and are still published all over the world. He is considered to be the father of the modern fairy tale.

About the Retelling Author

After working more than 10 years as a children's book editor, Stephanie True Peters started writing books herself. She has since written 40 books, including the New York Times best seller *A Princess Primer: A Fairy Godmother's Guide to Being a Princess*. When not at her computer, Peters enjoys playing with her two children, hitting the gym, or working on home improvement projects with her patient and supportive husband, Daniel.

About the Illustrator

Michelle Lamoreaux was born and raised in Utah. She studied at Southern Utah University and graduated with a BFA in Illustration. She likes working with both digital and traditional media. She currently lives and works in Cedar City, Utah.

THE HISTORY OF THE Princess -AND THE- Pea

"The Princess and the Pea" was first published in Copenhagen, Denmark, in 1835. It was printed in a small booklet titled *Tales Told for Children* along with three other fairy tales that Hans Christian Andersen had written.

Andersen's fairy tales were aimed at children, so they were less formal and poetic than other ones. Literary critics in Denmark disliked his versions. However, Andersen was confident that his tales would "win over future generations."

Many versions of "The Princess and the Pea" exist throughout the world, and some are stranger than others.

In an Italian version of this fairy tale, called "The Most Sensitive Woman," a prince must choose one of three princesses to be his wife. The prince decides to pick the third princess when she says a falling flower petal fell on her foot and injured her.

Hans Christian Andersen's version of "The Princess and the Pea" has been made into plays, ballets, musicals, and television and radio shows many times. It is one of the world's best-known fairy tales.

Discussion Questions

1. When the king answers the door, he finds a girl who says she's a princess. Did her story seem believable to you? Why or why not?
2. This story is a fairy tale. What are some other fairy tales? Which one is your favorite?
3. Do you think the queen's test was fair? Why or why not?

Writing Prompts

1. The prince and the princess end up liking a lot of the same things. Write about a friend or family member who you have a lot in common with.
2. The bedroom where the princess stays has a huge stack of mattresses. If you could design your dream bedroom, what kinds of things would you put in it?
3. Imagine that the princess failed the queen's test. What are some other ways she could prove she's a real princess?

approval (uh-PROOV-uhl)—if you give approval of someone, then you think he or she is acceptable or good

beggar (BEG-er)—a poor or homeless person who asks others for money or food

bouquet (boh-KAY)—a bunch of picked or cut flowers

delicacy (DEL-i-kuh-see)—if someone has delicacy, he or she is fragile or sensitive

exchanged (eks-CHAYNJD)—traded one thing for another

fled (FLED)—ran away from danger

illuminated (i-LOO-muh-nate-id)—brightened or lit up something with light

insisted (in-SIST-id)—demanded something very firmly

promising (PROM-iss-ing)—if something is promising, it is likely to turn out well

sensitivity (sen-suh-TIV-i-tee)—if someone has sensitivity, he or she is delicate or easily affected

ungrateful (uhn-GRATE-fuhl)—not thankful or appreciative of something

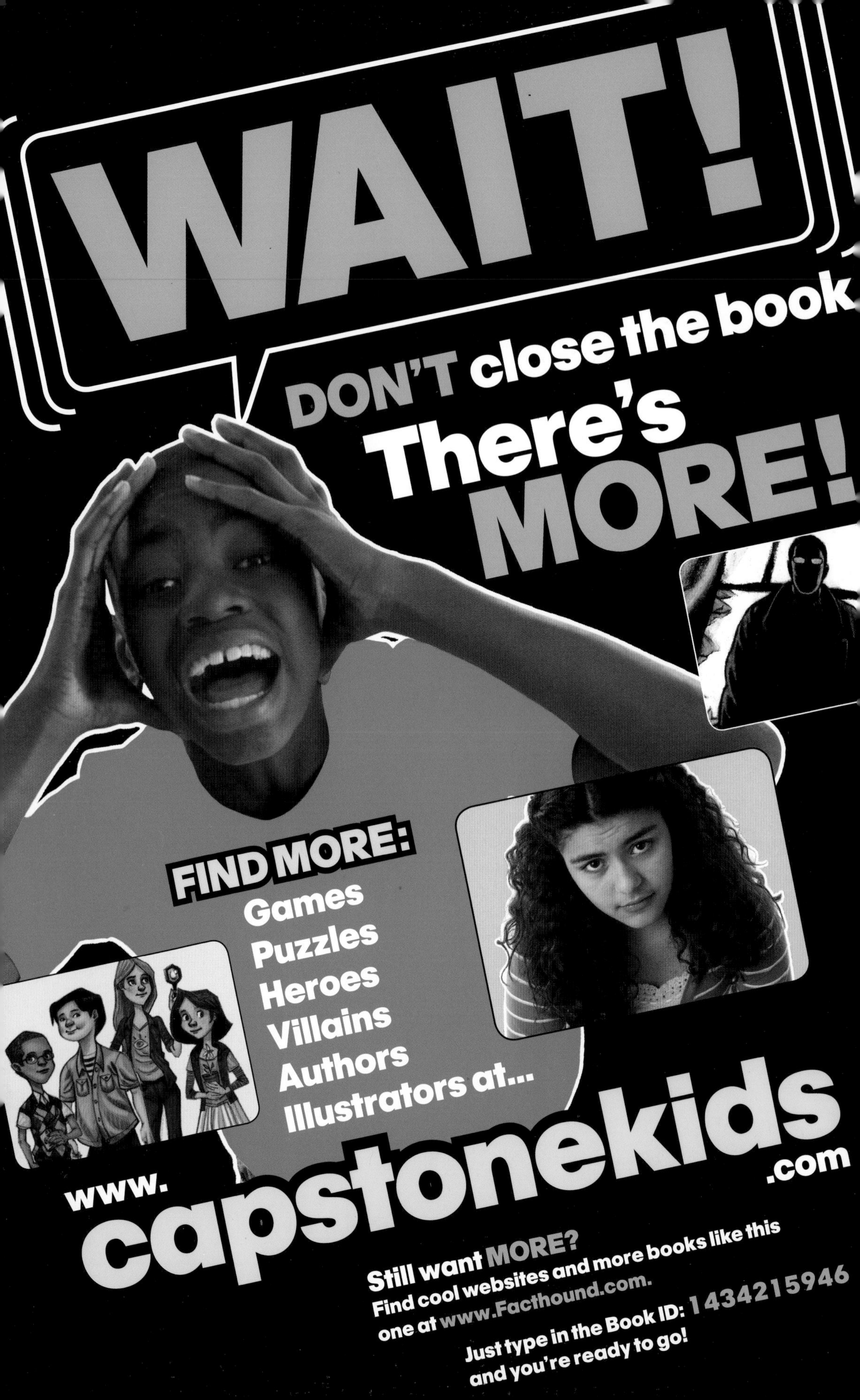
WAIT!
DON'T close the book
There's
MORE!
FIND MORE:
Games
Puzzles
Heroes
Villains
Authors
Illustrators at...
www.
capstonekids
.com
Still want MORE?
Find cool websites and more books like this
one at www.Facthound.com.
Just type in the Book ID: 1434215946
and you're ready to go!